The Case Of : Amy Black
Author and Illustrations

By: John Sylvester

@ by John Sylvester 2020 copyrights All right reserved. No part of this book may be reproduced, stored in a retrieval system or transmitted in any form or by any means without the prior written permission of the publishers, except by a reviewer who made "brief passages in a review to be printed in a newspaper, magazine or journal. Printed in the United States of America.

ISBN.   9798633816150

Book A

Dedication

I dedicate this book to all the people who are coping with the Covid-19 Isolation order.

Special thanks to Frances Sylvester who encouraged me since my youth to love writing.

This book evolved from two prior publications. It is a continuation of the saga.

Murder in Franklin County, Las Vegas, Nevada. These books

brought enjoyment to all who read them.

The Case of Amy Black is another proud writing by John Sylvester. Amy is the main character in "Clark County Murders."

I hope you find this book enjoyable.

Synopsis

The story begins in Nashville Tennessee. Two brothers looking for their Mother. Amy Black went to Las Vegas after a phone call accepting a job.

Amy was a 54-year-old African-American female. She was unmarried. She served several years in the Indiana Woman's Penitentiary.

She been missing for a month and a half. Her two Sons haven't heard from her. They live with her mother Emily Black. She filled a missing person report.

Months have passed. Not a word from the Police Department. The Covid-19 virus was starting to hit the nation.

It started in China and was spreading throughout the world. The president had put a stay at home order over the entire country. There was no travel allowed.

It was impossible for her to look for Amy. Mrs Black hired a private detective. He will investigate her disappearance.

Scott Taylor was a detective assigned to her case. He served as a Police Officer on different departments in the past twenty years. He retired and opened his own agency. The Taylor Agency.

He's been in private practice for six years. He has solved many missing person cases. Mrs. Black told him about Amy. He agreed to find her. He traced Amy's travels to Las Vegas, Nevada. Unknown to him he discovered a series of murders. They took place in Vegas involving four different people.

This story is about Felons involved in the disappearance of Amy. This book will explain how Taylor cracked the case. He had a difficult task because of Covid 19.The circumstances are very serious. Discover the outcome in these pages.

Introduction

The book opens in the office of Scott Taylor in February 2020. Scott's is on the phone having a conversation with the Indiana Police Department.

The conversations is in regard to Amy Blacks disappearance. He was making arrangements to pick up old files to help in the investigation. This has been ongoing for quite some time. The case has gone cold.

Scott became involved after receiving a phone call from Mrs. Emily Black.

She explained how her daughter disappeared. Sandra Burns called with a job offer from Vegas. She lives there. Amy was asked to meet her. She packed up and left excited about working in Nevada. She boarded a plane that evening and hasn't been heard from since.

Scott asked how Amy knew Sandra. Mrs. Black explained to him,

"Amy met Sandra through her daughter Clara. Amy and Clara were in jail together.

When Amy got out she wrote letters to Clara. The two of them hooked up after she was released. She was introduced to Clara's Mother some time after that. The three of them became good friends. Sandra moved to Las Vegas after her daughters death."

"Did she make arrangements to meet Amy at the airport?". Scott asked.

" No! Sandra was in the hospital. There were two other gentleman that picked her up. I believe their names were Seth and Carl. They both worked at the Casino."

"She wasn't too sure what the name of the casino was. Amy

never discussed her private business."

"Do you have the phone number to this Sarah Burns?" He asked Emily.

"I have a few different numbers I could give you." She replied.

"Who would they be for?" Scott inquired .

"Sandra. This is the casino number for Carl and Seth.

They will help you find her."
She said.

"Yes! Mrs Black. Any information I uncover will help your daughter. Is there anything else you can tell me?" He asked.

She told him about the ship with a Casino.

"I didn't know exactly what Amy was talking about. She had mentioned this. Amy's two sons Bert and Brett left for Las Vegas on Wednesday. They are in their 20's and members of a black gang.

They said,"They're going to the Casino to find their Mother. I believe there is going to be trouble. I couldn't stop them! I tried! They didn't care how they obtained the information. That's what scares me!" She said.

"They're old enough to take care of themselves. Don't you

worry about them Mrs Black. I'm going to be boarding a plane myself. I have to go to Vegas to close this investigation.

That's the only way. I hope I can get a flight out due to the Covid -19. Most flights were suspended.

Thank you for the information. I also obtained information from the Police. If you think of anything else you have my number. Give me a call." He told her.

"I will do that! Have a great day! Call me if you hear anything. Bye Scott." She hung up the phone.

(Act 1). A few hours after speaking with Mrs. Black Taylor phoned Sandra.

The phone rang. A woman answered.

"May I help you?" She said.

"Yes! Mrs Burns! I'm a private investigator. Taylor is the name. I'm calling you in regards to the disappearance of Amy Black. There's a few things I'd like to ask you. Do you have some time to speak?" He inquired.

Sandra hesitated and a frightening feeling came over her. She hesitated then said.

"I really don't think there's much I can help you with. What's the question?"

"Why did you invite her be down to Las Vegas? Was it for a job or something personal? Can you answer that?" He asked.

"I asked if she would be interested in working at the Casino. I had a friend looking for somebody to fill a position at the Casino. She came down to interview while I was in the hospital.

I had an accident and didn't get to see her. Only for a few minutes when she visited. I don't know what happened to her. There's nothing more that I could tell you." She told Scott.

"Can I get the names of person or persons she spoke to at the Casino? Plus the name of the Casino. Any other information? Try to center your thoughts to the day she arrived." Scott asked.

"I believe she spoke with Seth. It was the Poker House Casino. I don't have any other information." She replied.

"Thank you very much Mrs. Burns. I'll be flying down there in a few days. Would you mind if I dropped in on you? Can you give me your address please?" He asked.

"You have my number. Give me a call when you're down here. I'll give you my address then. I can't talk any longer."She hung up the phone.

Scott knew that she was lying. He sensed a bit of deception.

"What is she hiding?" He said to himself.

"She knows more than she's telling me. I'm gonna get it out of her face-to-face. I'll have to fly there."

He hit the intercom and asked his secretary to come in to his office.

"Rachelle can you please book a flight to Vegas for me. Tomorrow morning would be fine. Get back to me a soon as possible." He told her.

"I will try and get you a flight out in the morning. I don't think it's going to be easy. Most of the flights have been canceled because of Covid-19.

Most citizens were coming down with the Covid-19 Virus. Their stopping all the flights out of the airport. I'll see what I can do! I could book a private plane as a last resort."She told Scott.

He called the Casino to speak with Seth. He was unavailable.

They paged him but he didn't answer. His assistant answered the page. He was on another line with Sandra. She called and warn him about Taylor.

She told him, "Scott was coming to Vegas."

Seth told her, "Just relax and act normal."

"I had no information. I was in the hospital and knew nothing what-so-ever. That's all I told him."

"Good job! Stick to that story and I'll take care of the rest."Seth told her.

"I know you'll throw him off track Seth. You're good at that. Call Charles and warn him. I have to go". She hung up the phone.

(Act 11). Seth left Tennessee on the 9:45 Am plane to Vegas. There was a lay-over in Missouri. He arrive in Vegas at 8:45 the following morning.

Upon his arrival he checked into a Motor Inn. He was lucky to have booked a room. Most motels were closing due to the Covid-19 Virus.

The president was on national television. He ordered all businesses to shut down. It was a total stay at home order. Most of the restaurants and activities were closed. This wasn't going to halt his investigation.

He was stuck in the room for quite some time. He tried working on the phone but without success. Best thing to do was to wait it out. He sat in the motel for weeks.

During the shut down Seth was doing paperwork. Most of the employees were off. Many of them were laid off.

Sandra and Charles were working during the dilemma. There was a sanitation crew going over every piece of equipment in the Casino. The rugs were being shampooed and the windows were being washed.

The place was totally sanitized because of the Virus. Many people in Vegas came down with the Covid-19. There was an epidemic reaching out around the world.

So many people had died. Thousands were in the hospital. They were makeshift hospitals made in every Country around the world. It was a world epidemic.

Sandra had completed her work for that day. She told everyone she was leaving. She clocked out and proceeded to the garage.

She took the elevator to her floor. It was located below the main floor. As she exited the elevator she seen two men following her. She could hear footsteps behind her. She sped up to get to her car. As she did the sounds of walking became more rapid and aggressive.

She arrived at her car and opened the door. Once inside she started it. She noticed a couple of strangers coming towards her car. She put the car into drive and sped out of the parking lot.

The two males chased the car on foot towards the exit. Sandra was petrified. She didn't know who would follow her.

She picked up her cell phone. She called Seth, "I am being followed." She told him. They were waiting for me in the garage. I'm scared to death."She told him.

"Go home and call the Police. I will leave now. I will be there shortly. Lock the doors." Seth told her.

He called Charles on the intercom and told him to come to his office. Charles arrived in a few minutes. Seth told him what was happening to Sandra.

The two of them went down in the elevator to the garage. They sped off in the car and went directly to Sandra's house.

Seth had phoned the police. Sandra arrived in front of her home. There was a squad sitting in front. The police had arrived before her. She pulled into the lot and parked. The officers walked up to her car and opened the door. She got out.

" Are you Sandra Burns?" An officer asked?

"Yes! I'm Sandra!" She replied. I'm so glad you're ok. The Officer responded.

"I'm scared to death! So scared it's sickening me?" She said.

"What happened?" The officer asked.

"I came off the elevator at the Casino on Main Street. There were two black man waiting for me. I stepped off the elevator and they followed me to my car.

I got in the car and lock the doors. I started it and drove

away. As I drove away they chased me on foot. The exit gate closed in front of them as I drove off. It stopped them in their tracks." She explained.

"Let's go inside. I'll take a report up in side and file it at the station. You'll be getting a case number and my business card. We will escort you in." The officer told her.

It wasn't too long after they escorted her upstairs that Seth and Charles arrived. She open the door and let them in. They stood by the entrance.

The officer said to them," Hold off a minute guys."

She introduced them to the officers.

"How are they involved?" He asked.

She told him," No! Not at all. I just called them. They told me they were coming over".

"Did you get a good look at these men?" The officer asked.

"All I know is they were two black gentleman. They look like they were in their 20s. About 5'9". The two of them were dark skin one was a little lighter. They had dark blue jeans with white gym shoes and hoodies. That's all I seen as I sped out the gate. I noticed them from the rearview mirror." She said.

The officers asked her a few more questions. They completed their investigation and went downstairs to the squad. They told her they would be back with a copy of the report.

A few minutes passed and one of the officers knocked at the door. He handed her the report.

 He said, "If you have any further trouble please call the

department. "Goodbye" And walked away.

The three of them had a short conversation about the incident. While they were sitting the phone ring. Sandra stared at the phone. She was petrified to answer it. Seth picked up the phone and said,"Hello".

Whoever it was hung up. Seth got a frightened look covering his face. Their mouths dropped as they looked at each other.

"Who could that be?" Seth asked.

"I have no idea". She responded.

"Somethings up Charles! Seth said.

"Are you going to be ok here alone?" Seth asked Sandra.

" I don't know! I'm am scared to death." She replied.

Seth said, "Come home with me!"

The three of them left the building together. Seth and Sandra went to his home. Charles went back to the Casino.

(Act 111). The next day Scott called Sandra's phone. He made an appointment to visit with her. He arranged to meet her at 5 pm at her house. Sandra didn't want to meet with him alone.

She was accompanied by Seth. The two of them returned and waited. When Scott arrived they opened the door. He walked in and introduced himself.

Scott was quite surprised that Seth was there. When he walked in Seth was standing by the window overlooking the main drag. Sandra was walking around with a drink in her hand. She asked him to have a seat. He sat down he took out a ledger.

He said,"I need answers for various questions about Amy."

Sandra answered them the same way she did before. "I

don't know anything more than what I've told you."

Scott turned and looked at Seth. He said," Seth aren't you the gentleman that interviewed Amy?

He replied, "Yes! I interviewed and hired her".

"What was her position?" Scott asked.

"She took Sandra's place at a Casino party. It was on a

Cruise Ship. We needed a fill in on ship. She accompanied me there. She took Sanders place. Sandra was going to work the party but she had an accident.

She was in the hospital and I was in a spot. I was short help. Santa recommended her. I flew her in and took her on board." Seth explained.

"Did she return with you?" Scott asked.

"No! She didn't. She stayed an extra day on board with Carl to clean. I haven't seen either one of them since. They never came back. We filed a report in Florida."

"Do you know where they are? Is this why you're asking questions." Seth said.

"We believe something happened to them Seth. I don't know what . I was hired by Amy's mother to find her. It's become very hard to investigate this case with this pandemic. But I'm doing my job that's why am here." Scott explained.

While they were talking Scott happen to stand up. He look out the balcony window. He seen a gray sedan sitting out front with two black males. He didn't say anything to Sandra. He didn't want to scare her. Earlier Sandra had explained how she was followed. Scott knew those had to be the same men.

Scott figured if they seen him go out the door they might follow him. That would be perfect. It would get them away from the building. Then he would ditch them down the road. Scott excuse himself.

He said, "He would be in touch. Then said goodbye." He walked out the door.

He walked down the stairs to the front door. He opened it and the two gentlemen stared at him. He walked to his car ignoring them and got in. He started it and pulled away. They turned the lights on and followed him.

Scott was able to speed away from them. He ditch them with a little speed. They couldn't keep up with him. They had a rental car. The car had a small engine. Scott was driving a big V8 ex cop cruiser.

Scott made it back to the motel. He pulled in the

parking lot and got out. As he was walking to his room the sedan appeared. It came at him at a high rate of speed over the sidewalk.

The passenger started shooting. They shot the windows out of the cruiser. Scott's got up and fire back. The back window was blown out of their car. He watch as they sped away. He knew who they were. The Black brothers.

The stay at home order in Vegas caused the streets to be vacant. Many people were getting the virus. New York, Washington,California and Chicago were the hardest hit in the United States. Many people were expected to die.

The streets were vacant due to the restrictions in place. It was easier for Scott to walk around and spot Blacks car. He knew the Black brothers were a severe danger.

He had to investigate Amy's disappearance and watch his back. The job has becoming much harder than he signed up for. The virus helped. It cleared the streets.

Things were quiet during the morning. Scott got up and went downstairs for breakfast. He walked down the street and arrived in front of the Casino. Scott knocked on the door. Seth came to the door and unlocked it. He invited him in and locked the door behind him.

Scott told him about the Black brothers. He didn't say anything to them the night before. He wasn't sure it was them. Once they chased him he was sure.

Scott was unaware that Paul was really Charles. He was able to talk to Paul about the cruise. Paul and Steve had a discussion with him. Scott was asking more questions then they wanted to answer.

He demanded answers to questions about Carl. Scott asked for Carl's home address. Seth gave him the address. Scott left. He went to visit Carls widow.

Scott phoned her first. They set a time for him to visit. In the meantime Scott called the Las Vegas Nevada Police Department. He went in and seen Detective Allen. He was assigned to the case.

The two of them sat and had a discussion . Officer Allen told Scott he's going to set a trap. The news was to broadcast they found Carl's body. This would bring whoever killed him forward. It would bring his murderer to justice.

Scott made it to Carl's house and told her of the broadcast. They sat and waited for the news to finish. He needed every bit of evidence he could gather. The broadcast hit the television.

In the meantime Carl's wife had told Scott about the house. She told him Seth bought that house for some peculiar reasons. She could never figure it out. It rose Scott's radar. What would they want with an abandoned house.

Carl's wife did not know where the house was. Scott

questioned her over and over but she denied it. She was a very nice woman and worried about her husband.

She had filed a police report with the Nevada department. They haven't said anything to her. She knew they were working on it. It was good news when Scott told her he went to the department. At least she knew they were on the case.

After the broadcast Scott went back to the station. He sat down and spoke with Allan. They decided they would drive out to Sandra's.

They left the station and went into the cruiser. They arrived in front of her apartment. She happen to spot them out of the window. They got out and walked to the entrance door. They took the stairway to her apartment.

Sandra open the door with a nice greeting. Scott once again introduced himself. He also introduced the Allen.

Sandra was petrified. She had seen the broadcast about Carl. She knew they were going to talk to her about him. The three of them sat in living room and the question began.

Sandra broke down. She couldn't helping. She told them the truth. The questions were getting to her. She started with the day she rented her apartment. She said she was at the casino. Carl and Seth wanted to speak with her. She went up to the office.

The three of them sat and talked about a plot to murder Paul the owner. They wanted the money and the Casino. She was not going to participate in the plot. They convinced her with money. She agreed.

Scott asked her exactly how the plot played out. Sandra begin disclosing the details. They couldn't believe what she was telling them. What was about to be unfold was a gory murder. She went on telling them how Seth threw her into the cesspool.

(Act 1V). The story she told went as follows. Seth disclose that they wanted to murder Paul. The plotted this when they arrived in Vegas. They loved the money and the people.

They devised this plan to kill Paul. They would dump him in Bermuda. They wanted her to push Paul in a wheelchair. Amy wheeled his dead body onto the Ship. Charles killed him and hung him by his feet before boarded the ship. They hired some doctor to embalm him.

The next day Sandra has an accident. When she became disabled she couldn't participate. The two of them came to her. They asked her if she knew anybody to take her place. She recommended Amy. Seth called her and introduced himself. Amy came down to Las Vegas and she was ready to go.

She said the three of them murdered Paul. Charles took the place of Paul. They hired a plastic surgeon to reconstruct Charles face. They turned Charles into Paul to replace him on the ship.

The two officers sat there and listen . They couldn't believe horror story. It was an unbelievable tale.

She told them how Charles befriended Paul. Took on all

his traits. His likes and dislikes. He became acquainted with his friends. He had to do this to take over his life. When they felt confident. Charles was able to play his part and they proceeded.

That's all I can tell you about Paul. I know he was hung by his feet after they killed him. The Surgeon embalmed him. I don't have any more information about Amy.

What they did with her and Carl only God knows. When they were back Seth called. He told me they killed the two of them. I have no idea what happened to them or how.

I was in the hospital all the time. I know I conspired with them but I didn't act it out. The most you can charge me with conspiracy. Please don't let them know that I snitched them out. I am petrified of police officers and jail time. That's why I opened up because I knew Scott would get to the bottom this. It was just a matter of time before you found out.

The officer asked her to stand up and they handcuffed her. The three of them sat in the cruiser. The officer drove to the police department. She was fingerprinted and brought to the interrogation room.

Sandra was detained at the police station for a few hours. She had one charge at this time. The charge was conspiracy to commit murder. She posted bond and was released but was told not to leave the State pending further charges.

They had to conclude the investigation with the other gentleman. The Department would be back in touch with her. Sandra was ordered to stay away from them it was a condition of her release.

Scott was happy he found out what happened to Amy and Carl. He planned on going back to Carl's widow and telling her the story. The only other thing was to find the bodies.

They were not going to tell the others involved. If they found out they would disappear. Scott figured they would come up with a story that would clear them.
Scott left the police department and went to Carl's

widow. She open the door and let him in. He sat her down and told her. She started crying and screaming as he held her.

She was happy that she found out. It brought closure to the death. They sat for a while and spoke of Carl. It was getting late and Scott was exhausted. He excused himself and left. He was on his way back to the motel when the phone sounded.

He's phone rang . The call was from Sandra who was driving. She was being followed by the Black gentleman again. He asked her where she was and told her to drive towards the Casino.

She was told to drive into the parking area. Make sure they continue following you. She did as instructed. Scott waited at the entrance as he seen Sandra approach.

She quickly turn left into the parking area as followed behind her. Scott started the car and put it in drive.

He caught up to the Blacks brothers car. She laid down on the front seat. The two of them drove around to another aisle. Out the gate they went as Scott chased after them.

Scott followed them onto Main Street. They were driving at speeds exceeding 75 miles an hour making there get away. Scott called Officer Allen and gave him their location. The Police came quickly performing a pit maneuver to stop the brothers.

The little sedan swerved into the ditch. Three squad cars surrounded it as the police drew their guns.

"Ya'll put your hands up! Get out of the car." The Officer instructed.

Another officer walked around the side of the car as he aimed his gun to the passenger.

"Put your hands up! He shouted. They open the door and laid on the ground as they listened to the instructions without incident.

The officers handcuff them and they were taken into custody and seated in the cruiser.

(Act V).   Scott follow the cruiser to the station. When they arrive the two detainees were lead into the interrogation room. Scott joined the interrogation. The Officer opened door and the two brothers and Scott entered.

They were told to take a seat at the table. Scott follow and sat down.

Scott informed them he knew who they were. He also told

them they were stupid to come to town. Your Mother mentioned that both of you left Indy headed for Vegas last Wednesday."

The police officer entered the room. He sat down and looked at them.

"Are you guys crazy?" He asked.

They looked at him in surprise and shook their heads.

"You two could've gotten killed tonight. Do you know how many lives you put at risk. You were lucky that the streets were clear. You would have killed somebody if it wasn't for the Covid-19 pandemic. Main street is always busy. "

What are you two up to? Why are you in Las Vegas?" He asked.

Scott interrupted. "These are the sons of Amy Black!" He said.

"You two are under arrest for reckless driving that's for starters. We have a complaint filed against you for stalking. And last but least the gun fight last night with Scott.

These are all Felonies. We know where your Mother is you can stop looking for her. She was murdered." The two of them broke into tears.

"What happened to her?" One of them asked.

"It's still an open investigation. We can't disclose information about her. We have one of the suspects in custody. The investigation is on going there are other suspects involved.

You're going to get booked tonight. We need to get you into fingerprint room and take your pictures and prints. Get up you guys. He instructed. I need to take your handcuffs off."

The two of stood and turned around as the officer took the key one by one and he unlocked the cuffs. He waved at the officer through the glass of the door. He opened the door and signal them to follow him. They did as he instructed as they walked out the door.

Scott was told not to let out what they've learned. He

didn't want anybody to know about Sandra's confession.

It would take a few days but they were going to investigate the Casino including everyone that work there. They also needed to investigate what happened on the ship with Paul.

Scott told him that he will help them confirm the deceased was Amy. It was getting late and he needed rest. Scott left the station and drove to the motel.

(Act V1).   The next day Allen and Scott began working on the case. They called the Indiana Department of Corrections.

Scott inquired about arrest records on Charles Cooper. They requested the State send the files including all his criminal information.

Allen called the British Country of Bermuda. Officer Parkman answered the call. Allen gave him Seth's information. They asked for records about the house. The records were forwarded via fax.

Seth called the Department of Medical Records. He wanted Paul's fingerprints, dental records. He ran his social security number through the records department.

The police records indicated he had prior arrests which included an arrest for money laundering by the FBI. They continue to investigate. Allen asked those records be forwarded to him. It took a few days for gather all the files.

Allen and Scott went into a conference room and carried it some files. One by one they started going through them. They recorded all the pertinent information and ignored the rest.

They had evidence they required to arrest Charles .

Allen had a stake out put on the Casino. They followed Charles and Seth.

They were hoping one of them to lead them to the house. Carl's wife didn't know the location. It was vital to the investigation it was located.

Alan sent a squad to pick up Paul. The Officers knocked on the Casino door. Seth answered door. "Can I help you?" Seth asked.

The officers responded, "We're looking for Paul is he in?"

"Yes! Seth said.

He moved out of the way as he pointed up the stairs. First room on the right is Paul's office. They followed the instructions but the door was closed. The officers knocked.

  "Come in." Someone responded.

The officers opened the door and walked in. Charles was shocked. He couldn't believe cops were standing in front of him. "What do you guys want?"

" Charles Cooper?" The Officer asked.

"No! My name is Paul!" He replied.

"The game is over Charles stand up! The police stood behind him. He told Charles to turn around and he did. The officer grabbed his arms and cuffed him. They walked him to the cruiser and he was put inside.

Charles was lead to the investigation room. He was told to sit at a table. Officer Allen went to grab the paperwork while Scott sat with him. Allen came back with a handful of records. He handed Scott a notepad.

"The game is over Charles we found Carl. Your friend Sandra snitched you out. We know who you are. We need to confirm that though." Allen said.

Charles had no response. He just sat there starred.

"Charles, we know you were arrested in Indiana. You did time in the state prison. I want you to explain the events that led up to the arrest. This will help verify you are Charles. It could be that your somebody else. What happened that you landed in prison?" Allen asked.

He looked at the officers in disbelief. He turned to Allen and said, "I am Charles! I'm caught! I will describe the events." He said.

"I'm schizophrenic. I was in a juvenile detention center when I was younger and living with my grandfather. When I was released from the detention center I was an adult. My grandfather did not want me back at the house.

I had this girlfriend. Her name is Clara Burns. She is Sandra's daughter. Her and I moved the Stark County Indiana and rented a house on Bass Lake.

I drove a truck making deliveries. On my route I would visit small towns and rob the store owners. I got away with it for quite some time. There was a day I took

Clara with me and my life changed.

Clara was unaware that I packed a gun. I remember pulling into a small town and we stopped at a gas station. I planned on robbing it. I didn't know Clara was going to follow me in. She went into the ladies room.

I told the cashier to open the drawer and handover the cash. While he was collecting the cash, Clara came out of the bathroom. I wasn't unaware there was a state policeman in the store.

Clara spotted him when she came out of the bathroom. She happen to notice the gun in my hand. Is that the owner. She shouted out,

"Charles!Charles! there's a cop! Put the gun down. I turned around and both guns fired. The officer missed me but I got him. I knew that was the end of my freedom. The officer was hit with a bullet in the chest. The sounds of the gunfire rang out as folks started running.

The officers uniform beginning to show signs of the open wound. Blood was seeping through his shirt. He raised his hand and grabbed his chest in agony. He began screaming as the feeling of pain worsened. There was a pause and he fell to the floor.

The attendant phoned the police as I ran out the door. I stood outside knowing I lost my freedom. There were cops all over the place. That's how I went to the penitentiary. I left the customers in total horror. The Officer died a few hours later.

Carla was pissed because she was arrested. She didn't expect me to do what I did. She was in shock and proclaimed her innocence. The police didn't believe her version. The lawyers told her it was going to be a long time before she got out. I got 11 years and so did she.

Alan was going over his previous arrest records. The story Charles told matched the files and the reports. Allen looked up and said, "Charles I believe you."

Charles looked at him and responded. "There is no reason for me to lie".

"You're right! Allen responded. I need one more thing from you. I need the information on the murders in Vegas. Let's see if your story matches Sandra's. If you're totally honest with me I'll cut you a deal."

Charles begin to speak. I was at home in Tennessee and Sandra called me. She left a message for me to call her back. She met me at a restaurant across the street from the place I was staying.

She said, "I'm moving to Vegas with you.

"She told me she had two friends that were planning a murder and take over casino. There was a lot of money involved. It was quite impressive and I'd liked the plot. I agree and we flew back to Vegas.

When we got the Vegas. She introduced me to Carl and

Seth. We met up in the casino. I believe it was in the restaurant. It could've been in Seths office. Anyway, they told me about the plans to kill this Casino owner.

 I would have to become friends with him and would need to learn everything and anything about him. It would take a while. I would have to know his friends and all his habits. I was to take over his life. Sandra told me I was the correct built to replace him.

Seth hired a plastic surgeon and look what he done. I have a handsome face again. It was a few weeks after that. The plan was to move forward. There was a Casino night on this ship. It was leaving for Bermuda from Florida. That ship is owned by the Casino.

It was departing from Florida on Friday night for the Fourth of July weekend. On Wednesday, Seth and Carl brought Paul to an abandon house.

It's an old condemned place out in the country. I don't know exactly where it's at but Seth owns it. I was waiting inside behind the door with a rope in my hands.

They walked in with Paul. When they open the door I jumped out and strangled him until he fell to the floor. They carried him down to the basement and hung him by his feet from the rafters.

He was ready for the plastic surgeon to embalm him. A slash to his wrist drained the blood out. Someone was there to help him. I don't know who it was.

The next day Carl and Seth went to the house and cut him down. They loaded him in a wheelchair and put him in the back of a rented van. The two of them drove to Florida to meet Sandra at the ship.

In the meantime Sandra had an accident and couldn't do her part. She was going to wheel the dead body up into the ship and into the cabin. She was in the hospital. I don't know how they found the other female named Amy Black.

Seth hired her and brought her in from Tennessee. She put on a nurse uniform and took over Sandra's job. By pushing the wheelchair with the stiff. When the ship got to Bermuda she brought it off the same way.

What they did after that I don't know. I was waiting in the house in Bermuda. I was accompanied by two contractors. They dug a 6 foot hole where the addition was being built. The body was going to be put into the hole and buried.

They arrange for the concrete to be poured the next day. That's it. When the three of them arrived they dumped the body and we went back to the states.

"Are you trying to tell me you only killed Paul?" Allen asked"

"The only one that I was involved in." He responded.

"Who killed Carl? What happened to Amy?" Allen asked.

"I couldn't tell you. I wasn't involved in those murders. I went back to the casino after we go off the ship. That's something you're gonna have to ask somebody else. I told you everything I know. I swear! I swear!" Charles stated.

"You're a liar. You had something to do with the other murders. You need to tell me or you going to the chair. What happened to Amy and Carl?

You already confessed to the other murder. You might as well tell us. Let's have it Charles". Scott shouted loudly.

I'm not gonna say anything until I have an attorney present. I confessed to Paul's murder and I've been honest. I want to see an attorney. Take me to my cell." Charles stated.

"We will get you to a cell. We have to get your fingerprints and a mug shot. I'm waiting for someone to type your confession we need your signature. Then we'll book you. You have nothing more to say Charles?" Allen asked.

"Just a reminder Charles. If we find out later that you withheld information it isn't going to be good for you. The promises I made will be gone. Are you sure you have nothing else the tell us?" Allen repeated.

"OK I'll tell you about Amy. On the way back she sat in the back of the van. I'm talking about the cargo part in the back. Carl climbed back there with her and pulled out a gun with a silencer and shot her.

The three of us drove to the house I was told you about. Like I said, "I don't know where it is".

"We carried her down to the basement. We got rid of her the same way we did Paul. The three of us dug a hole and we dumped her in it.

I have a surprise for you. Carl and I were talking while Seth walked out to the van. Both of us couldn't figure out why. We stood there staring at Amy's body. It looked cold and so dead. Her hair had dirt over it. Her clothes became soiled as she hit the water and mud.

The hole was loaded with water to the bottom . She was submerged partially in the water. It was muddy and slimy.

I turned away. I couldn't stand looking at her any longer. It was a horrible thing that was done. Why Carl shot her I don't know. Seth came down the stairs and into the basement.

Carl was facing the hole looking at Amy. Seth walk up

and shot him in the back. Carl fell down into the hole on top of Amy.

The two of them laid there in the mud. It was a horrible sight as I freaked out. Seth pointed the gun at me.

"He told me you're going to be next. I don't need you. Are you going to keep your mouth shut?"

 "I was so scared he was going to shoot me. I told him I would do anything. It was at that time we talked about Paul's estate." Charles told them.

"We need to find the abandoned house. You have no idea where it's Located? Are you telling us the truth Charles? Where is the house?" Scott asked.

"I'm telling you. I don't know the streets in this town. It's condemned. It used to be a play house for prostitution . The men from the casino had sex there. This was years ago when the mob ran Vegas. This is what I was told.

Seth bought the house from Paul. I know what it looks like but after that I can't help you. I promise! I'm telling you everything I know!" Charles Said.

There was a knock at the office door. Allen turned around and signaled the officer to open the door. The officer stuck his head in the room.

"Officer Allen there's a phone call for you. It's urgent I was told. Can you excuse yourself from this meeting and take the call."

Allen excuse himself and went out the door. The desk officer handed him the receiver. He put it in his ear and said,

"Hello!" A mans voice responded.

"This is Dr. Hall from the Suburban Hospital. I'm calling you about Sandra Burns. She has Covid 19. She is in the hospital not doing too well. I have to keep her in a respirator. She will be confined here for at least 14 days.

To be honest with you officer I don't think she's going to make it. She's having a hard time breathing. Her age isn't favorable with this virus. Her lungs are collapsing.

I will let you in to talk to her if you need to. She said she has something she wants to tell you. Can you come out here?"The Doctor requested.

"I'm very sorry to hear that Dr. Hall. I'm so glad you called me. I need to find out information on a case I'm working on. Since she requested to see me. I have to come out.

I'm working on an interrogation at this moment. I will be there about 3:30 this afternoon. Will that be OK with you? I'll ask for you at the desk?" Allen said.

"Ask for me I will bring you to her . You will receive instructions so you won't get sick. It is very dangerous for you to come here. I am going to make an exception because this is very important.

When it involves a police investigation I can't refuse the officer. I'm going to have a plastic bubble put over her bed to protect you. I'll see you at 3:30."The doctor hung up the phone.

"Allen was very concerned about Sandra's health. He needed more information from her. He went back to the interrogation room. He peered through the glass door. Scott looked up towards him as Allen waved for him to come out in the hallway. Scott got up and open the door and walked out.

" What's up?" Scott's asked

" Sandra is in the hospital. She has the virus. The doctor called me. She wants to speak with me about this investigation. I guess she's has more to tell us. She has nothing to loose now.

Shes not doing too well. I told the doctor I'd be there about

3:30. I just wanted to give you heads up. We need to end this interrogation. Time to book this guy." Alan stated.

"That's horrible. She worked at that hospital. I understand why she has the virus. All these nurses and doctors are going to get sick. That virus is a horrible thing.

I feel we've gotten all the information we're going to get from Charles . We can always continue this another time.

Why don't you go ahead and book this guy..

You need to wait till his confession is typed. We're going to have to go back in there. It shouldn't be too much longer. In the meantime take him to be fingerprinted.

 They can do a new mug shot too. Once the confession is typed and signed we will be done. Then you can book him." Scott said.

"He requested to see an attorney before he signs that confession. We have him fingerprinted and have a mug shot done. Get that out of the way. Go book him. We're done here are you going to come to the hospital with me?" He asked.

"I guess so. I'd like to hear what she has to say. This is turning out to be much more than I signed up for. I can't believe all this.

These people are really warped in the head. Very interesting story though. Wouldn't you agree?" Asked Scott.

"I agree! Ok I'm gonna go in there and get this guy out of here. You sit tight for a bit". Allen told Scott.

They went back in the room. Allen escorted Charles into the hallway and took him to be processed. Scott went to the coffee machine and got a cup of brew. He returned to the interrogation room and sat there.

He wanted to keep distance from everybody in the office. The department didn't have too many officers at work. Most of them were out in the street but a handful stayed home.

Quite some time went by and Allen came back to the interrogation room. He waved through the glass for Scott to come out. The two of them walk down the hallway that led to the parking garage. They located the Cruiser and got in. They were on their way to the hospital which wasn't too far from the police station.

They arrived and park the car. Officer Allen called up to the nurses station from his phone. He alerted them they were coming up. They needed Doctor Hall to meet them.

They walk thru the parking lot and into the building. They entered the elevator and went to the isolation floor. The doctor was at the desk waiting.

He gave them instructions. They should keep their distance from Sandra. They were only allowed 15 minutes. Both of them walked into the room. Sandra was under a bubble with a ventilator running. It was hooked to the shield.

Allen tapped her foot and woke her. She opened her eyes and said, "Officer Allen!"

Both of the officers greeted her. Alan started speaking.

"You have something to tell me Sandra. I'm sorry to see you in this condition. If there is anything else yo about this investigation I need to know?

 Please! I need to know where the house is. There are two

houses involved. One is here in Vegas and the other in Bermuda . Where are they located?" He asked

Sandra slowly opened her eyes. She was very weak and pale and Egan to cough. She looked at them.

"The condemned house is at 5 N. Wells St. just outside of town. I need to tell you something more important Allen. Amy's and Carl's are buried at the house. They bury them in the basement. I don't know where the house in Bermuda is but Charles knows.

I have to tell you something else. I went to the house with the doctor. I helped him embalm Paul's body. I brought all the embalming equipment in while he was bloodletting. We cleaned everything up after he was done. We sat Paul up in the wheelchair preparing him to be moved.

That's what I needed to tell you. I'm not gonna be around much longer I have a high fever. I figured you might as well know. It's been bothering me since I bonded out. I wanted to come back and tell you but I got sick.

I can't live with myself . Maybe this is Gods answer. Satan is coming to take me. I deserve it. This is a horrible thing I am involved in. The lesson learned was greed for money isn't worth it.

I've lost a good friend because of it. I told Carl to kill Amy. Carl shot her in the back. I didn't want to split the money with her. Honestly. I swear! I swear!" She said.

"Thank you Sandra for telling us. I'm sorry there's nothing I can do for you and your illness. If you make it through this I will help you at court. I'll make sure you don't get the chair. We pretty well got this investigation wrapped up. I will have to book you again. I feel bad doing this but I must cuff you to the bed.

There will be a man watching your door out the hallway. Thank you very much. I hope you feel better. I'll check in with you in a few days. The two of them said goodbye and left."

The officers left the hospital. They were through for the Day. Scott went back to his room. Allen went to the station. They planed to meet in the morning.

They were taking a ride out to the house. The bodies have to be located. Arrangements for someone to come unearth the deceased had to be completed. This was going to be done the same day.

The morning came quickly. Scott had a good rest overnight. He got dressed and went to the police station. Allen was waiting for him.

They sat down in the office and discussed the case.

Allen informed Scott that they he had a warrant to pick up Seth. That was the first order of business. After that they were going to the house. They left the office and walked to the cruiser.

Seth was on the phone with Hilda. He was talking to her about the police. He informed her that they picked up Charles. She wanted to know what she told the police. Hilda is Carl's wife. No one knew but two of them were having an affair. They conspired this whole scam. That's why Carl was killed.

After they gained control of the casino Seth was to kill Sandra. They're little scam was over and Seths freedom was coming to an end.

Hilda said, " I have to get off the phone Seth".

"What?" Seth said.

"I said good luck and goodbye. It's over and I'm out of here." She hung up the phone.

Seth was shocked that she did that. She was done with him. He was in trouble and going to the penitentiary. The police were on the way. She was going to play innocent. She was going to tell the police that Seth was lying. She don't know what he's talking about.

When the call concluded Hilda packed a bag and walked out the door. She was leaving Vegas as she sat in the car and took off.

She was not answering anymore question. She didn't want to get arrested. She didn't know where she was going. She's just driving out of Las Vegas.

(Act V11).   The police arrived at the casino. Seth left the building. He was in the parking lot. He just sat in his car and started it. He put the car in drive and took off. Officer Allen happen to spot him. They proceeded to chase him.

They sped quickly out of town towards the desert. Seth was driving at a high speed. Allen called in ahead for some back up. He informed them of his location .

The other officers stopped ahead and put laid nail strips in the road. They were watching as Seth approached them. His two front tires hit them. Seth spun out and the car turned over. The police surrounded the vehicle.

They jumped out of their squad and open his door to save him. The engine started on fire. The car was totaled. They managed to pull him out. He was unconscious . They drag him away from the vehicle.

Allen called in for an ambulance. Before the ambulance got there Seth came to. He was in a shock stage but alert. He's eyes were open. Scott and Allen pick him up and sat him down inside the Cruiser . Allen told him he was under arrest for murder.

He started asking him questions about Amy. He was responsive and talking. The ambulance pulled up an the EMTs got out.

After careful examination they concluded that Seth was fine. He had a couple contusions and a broken rib but he would be ok. Allen was happy to hear that. He had a task for Seth to complete. He went to the cruiser and handcuffed him.

Allen called the tow truck. He noticed the truck coming up the road. The driver backed up towards the car.

He extended the cable and hooked it to the frame. He pull the car forward with the truck. It came upright an landed on all four. He unhook the car and backed up to the front of it. The wench pulled it onto the flat bed and the driver strapped it down. He was headed for the Police pound. The car became state property and was confiscated.

Scott an Allen returned to the cruiser. The three of them

headed out of town. They were taking Seth out to the house. Seth became nervous. He knew that Allen found out about the house. They pulled up in front. Seth looked at the front and recalled what happened inside. Allen turned towards the backseat and said to Seth, "Does this look familiar?"

"The game is over Seth! We know!" Allen told him.

Seth looked and noticed the squad cars parked on the grass. There were ambulances parked along the walkway. Policemen were everywhere around the home.

Allen went around to the rear passenger door and opened it. Seth stepped out of the squad . The three of them walked into the house. Seth was between Allen and Scott. They walked him down into the basement. There were men unearthing the corpuses .

Seth watch them unearthing the bodies. The officers knew they were getting close. A strange oder emerged from the soil. They dug a few more inches and Carl's arm appeared.

"Get down in the hole. Dig them out with your hands. Don't ruin evidence by hitting the deceased with those shovels. I want them intact as they are. The two men jumped down in the hole and started digging puppy style.

They were careful digging around Carl's body. They knew Amy was lying beneath him.

They cleaned soil off the bodies. The oder was unbearable. Seth couldn't believe what he was experiencing. He turned around and looked down at the ground. He began to vomit

The officers placed their handkerchiefs over their nose and mouth. Seth begged them to take him outside. Scott walked Seth up the stairs . Another officer followed them.

It took about three hours for them to totally unearth the two corpses. Seth was taken to the police station and booked. The bodies started to decompose. They were still intact. The coroner was examining them. Allen and Scott returned from the station. They where waiting for the coroner comments and discussing the case. They sat less than twenty minutes and the coroner came out the front door.

He didn't have a good look on his face. Behind him were two corpses on gurneys . The officers exited the car and walked up to him. They asked," May we speak a moment?"

The corner replied, "Yes! No problem! What do you need?"

"Cause of death? We're they shot?" Allen asked.

"Yes! Both bodies shot in the back. He replied . We are transporting them to the corners office for autopsy. I'll send you a full report in about a week." He replied.

"That's all we need to know. Thank you."They turned and walked to the car.

It was lunchtime. When they arrived at the station they ordered food. Their plan was to eat and then pull Seth into the interrogation room. They needed to get a statement from him.

(Act 1X). A snack was being served at the hospital. Sandra was accepted her tray. They placed it under her tent. She put the tray on her lap and began to eat.

While she was eating Doctor Oleo appeared. He was the same doctor that embalmed Paul. The two of them worked side-by-side in the laboratory. That's how she befriended him.

"How is Sandra this afternoon?" He asked.

"I'm not doing too well Dr. Oleo. I don't even feel like eating this meal. I'm glad you stopped up. I need to tell you something. The cops know everything. I've been trying to get the nurses to get you up here since yesterday." Sandra told him.

"You're kidding! How did they find out about it?" The doctor asked.

I really don't know how the investigation started. They came to me at my home. This was before I was sick. They knew everything about me. They were just up here today. I don't know what to tell you. But I wanted to warn you.

"Give me a few minutes Sandra. I'll be right back. I need to make a phone call." He turned and walked out of the room.

Dr. Oleo stepped out in the hallway. He looked around I noticed the storage room door. He walked towards it and opened it. There were towels and supplies in there but enough room for someone to get in. He went inside the room and close the door. He turned the light on. He took his cell phone out of his pocket and dialed a number. Hilda Franklin answer the phone. Carl's wife.

"Hilda this is Dr.Oleo. The cops are closing in! Did you know that? I'm here with Sandra. She told me what was going on. Where are you?" He asked.

"I know the cops are on to us. They were at my house twice. Seth called me and wanted me to run away with him. I told him he's on his own. I hung up the phone. I didn't want to stay at home.

"They arrested Charles yesterday afternoon. I believe he's still in jail. They found the bodies. Did you know that?" She said.

"I can help you Millie. I'm going to be going back to talk to Sandra. She's not gonna make it through this virus. I'm going to ask her to give me her license.

That license is a great benefit for you. If they come after you, I'll perform surgery and you will become Sandra. Don't worry about anything. I'll take care of this." He said to her.

"That would be so cool. Those cop will never find me. You have my number. Call me and let me know. I'll be staying at the Brookside Inn. If you need to get a hold of me. Thanks Doc! Good luck."She hung up the phone.

Dr. Oleo went back to Sandras room. She was done eating her snack. He reached under the tent and took the tray from her. He set it on the table.

 "Sandra, I need to ask you something. Would you be willing to give me your drivers license. It's for Hilda, Carl's wife. She's on the run.

"The cops know about her helping me. I'm going to perform surgery on her face. She will look like you and have identification. She'll be able to live the rest of her life. Can you help us?" He asked her.

"I know the end is coming. You can have my license. God bless her. It will be a few days before I'm gone. My lungs are full of contaminated fluid. I can't even breathe.

 This virus is horrible for anyone who gets it. I'm weak, vomiting and I can't breathe. It's the worst part of all of it. Go in my purse. The license is in my wallet." She said.

"I found it. Thank you so much Sandra. This is gonna be a big help. You're her only chance to have her freedom. Seth and her skimmed a bunch of money from the Casino." He said.

"All of us did a stupid thing. If I survive this I'm going to jail for a long time. I don't need a drivers license where I'm going. I know the cops are coming back in a few days to see how I am.

We'll take it from there. Go now and call her. Let her know you're going to help her. She has nobody since Carl is gone. Your good moral support for her. Go ahead! Get going and call her. I'll see you in a day or two." Sandra told the doctor.

The doctor said goodbye and excuse himself. He walked out the door.

Back at the police station. Allen took Seth out of lock up. He walked him into the interrogation room. Scott was waiting. The two of them sat down and started discussing the murders.

"He told Seth he needs a confession. He is facing quite a long sentence. If he confesses he will get a lighter sense." He agreed.

Seth began disclosing his involvement in the murders.

"It's really embarrassing that I have to come out with this. I was enticed by money and popularity. To be rich was something I always dreamed of as a boy.

Carl and I grew up together. As boys we were best friends. We spent all our time together as teenagers.

We met our wives in high school. We dated for a few years. Both of us got married.

The ladies were also best friends during those years. I was in love with Hilda. That was Carls wife. He had married her before I could separate them.

  I married Rhonda. Hilda and I devised this scam to gain ownership of the Casino. This whole plan was our idea. We spoke for months putting this together. We lived in Florida at the time. I had Hilda talk my wife into moving to Las Vegas. I did the same to Carl. It didn't take long for everyone to agree. We took the step and moved .

 Carl and I acquired a job at the casino. We went there because we were friends with Paul. When we traveled to Vegas we would dine with him. We became very close. It was in the plan.

 He offered us a job many times. Thats when I came up with the idea. I had to convince Carl. It was no problem he was game from the start.

I continued to have an affair with Hilda on the side. When Carl was working we would be going out eating and doing different things. During my working hours I met Sandra. She was quite a lady. Very smart and knew her game.

 I would sit and play roulette with her. We would both laugh and have a good time. I would buy her drinks whenever she came to Vegas. She was the perfect fish.

She was to wheel the dead body on and off the ship. The perfect person. She was a nurse and had access to a wheelchair and nurse uniform. Carl and I discussed her involvement and Carl agreed.

The next time Sandra came into the Casino I approached her. We had a meeting in my office. She agreed. The plot was in motion.

Everything was going great until Sandra got hit by a car. We had planned to do this on the Fourth of July. When she was hit we had to stop . Sandra came up with the idea of Charles and Amy. We thought it was great.

I knew that doctor and so did Sandra. He came into the Casino regularly. Sandra went back to Tennessee to move her furniture . She had rented a new apartment. She called

Charles and Amy. They both came to Vegas. Things were great again.

Carl and I lured Paul to the house. Carl and I acquired both houses for this plot. We needed the other house to bury Paul's Body. Charles was waiting behind the door.

 We walked in with Paul. He took a rope and strangle him. We carried him down the stairs into the basement and hung by his feet.

Charles had left. He had to catch a plane to Bermuda. He went to the other house and waited.

The Doctor and Sandra prepared the body for shipping. They embalmed him and put him in the wheelchair. That was the only involvement the Doctor had. This was done before Santa went to hospital.

Amy push the body on and off the ship.We rented a van and

drove it to the Bermuda house. Charles was waiting. The whole was dug and we dumped Paul inside. There were two British men that covered him up and poured cement over him.

We came back on the ship the same day. The van was parked in the lot. The four of us climbed into the van and rode to the house. Carl shot Amy on the way there. He put the gun against her back and pulled the trigger .

We arrived at the house. The. body was thrown into a hole the three of us dug. I went out and got the gun. When I came back I shot Carl in the back.

I wanted to be with Hilda. She called me earlier today and told me we were through. I couldn't believe that she dumped me. She wants out of here. I don't exactly know what she meant but I wanted to tell you.

She's the reason I shot Carl. I was going to divorce my wife. After they were buried we went on our way. That's the story in its entirety."

"You know you're going to book you for murder. Multiple murders. While we're on the subject what is the doctors name? Where does he work at? Is he here at the hospital?" Allen asked.

"Yes! He works right here on Cross Street. He's a surgeon in that hospital. Same hospital where Sandra worked. That's how we met him through her." Seth explained.

"We're done here Allen said. You can stand up. You're going to the cell block."

Allan directed him to the door. He opened it. He walked with him towards another officer. He took Seth to a cell.

Allan and Scott drove back to the hospital. They went there to look for Oleo. They walked to the desk and ask the nurse where he was .

She told them, "He was here but he's off duty . He must have left. I would say about a half hour ago. I guess he went home .

"We have to find this guy." Allen told Scott.

" I'll send a squad to pick him up. If they don't locate him I'll put APB out on him. Let's get back to the station." Allen said.

Once they arrive back at the station Allen went to check his messages. He went to his message box and there was a document in an envelope. He opened it and it was orders from the chief.

It ordered him to go to Bermuda and find the other house. He was ordered to locate the two contractors.

Allen closed the box and walked back over to Scott.

"I have orders to find the house and those contractors in Bermuda. You want to come along? I'm out of here in the am." He asked.

"I'll pass it on. I have reports to write up for my client. I have a few important things I have to do here before I go back to Tennessee.

Just keep me posted by phone. I won't leave till you get back. I have to find that doctor." He told Allen .

Scott went back to the motel. He open the door and went in and sat on the bed. He bent over and took his shoes off then laid down on the bed.

He put his face into the pillow. He just wanted to close his eyes and relax. He had rested about two hours and the phone rang. It was Officer Alan.

"Scott! I have some news for you! Sandra passed away at 2:13." He told him.

"That's a shame." Scott replied.

"I'm going over there now. I thought you would wanna

know. That's why I called. Do you wanna come with?" Allen asked him.

"I'll pass I'm exhausted. There's no reason for me to go there. Do your thing Allen." He said goodbye and hung up the phone.

Scott had a good rest that evening. When he rose in the morning he clothed and left the motel. He walked down to the car rental agency. He rented a car.

His first stop was Hilda Franklin's house. He was going to question her.

What was her involvement in these murders. He pulled to the side of the road and pulled out a note pad. He obtained her address and drove to her house.

Scott arrived at the house and park the car. It looked quiet. Know one was home. The blue sedan that was there last time was gone. He walked up to the door and knocked a few times.

He knew she wasn't in. He walked around through the bushes and looked in the windows. The house is totally empty. Just a few pieces of furniture scattered about. He knew she took off.

"Where did she go?"He asked him self. He knew it was a lost cause to look for her. His next step was to go find the doctor.

He was going to the hospital and get his home address.

He stopped up at the nurses office and obtained the information . Went back out to the car and proceeded to his house. It was about 14 miles south of town. He drove to the address.

He was surprised at what he seen as he rolled into the drive. It was a rolling estate with beautiful trees.

The house was a small mansion. There were workers outside trimming the lawn and cutting the bushes.

He drove up the long driveway. It curved around to the front of the house and back out to the road. He parked the car close to the workers. He turn the car off and got out.

He approached one of the workers that was cutting the grass. He tapped him on the shoulder and the guy stopped the motor on the mower.

The worker looked at him and got off the tractor.

"May I help you Sir?" He asked.

"Is the doctor home?" Scott asked.

The worker told Scott. " The Doctor packed a bag and left this morning. He hasn't seen him since 7:30 AM. There was some woman with him.

He left with her. I've never seen her before. He said he'd be back in a few days and pulled out of the drive."

"He didn't say where he was going?" Scott asked.

Scott drove over to the police station. He went inside and ask the Chief for an open desk.

He pointed to one he could use. Scott sat down and took out a pad of paper and pen.

The phone calls began. He was calling bus lines and plane reservations. He was trying to find where the Doctor had gone. He knew he had to be with Hilda . It was a few hours later he found them on a flight to Bermuda .

Scott got up and walked up to the Chief. He asked him."

What time Allen left for Bermuda".

" He's still in town. He will be leaving tonight. We had to delay his flight. He had to get paperwork to the hospital.

She is to be buried in the prison graveyard. She is custody of the state. There isn't going to be any private ceremony. He had to give them release papers."
"Thank you Chief! I'll call his cell phone". Scott reply.

Scott walked back to the desk and dial Allen's numbers. The phone rang a few times and he answered.

"Officer Allen?" He replied .

"This is Scott! I'm glad you haven't left yet. I have some information for you. Are you busy right now?"
He inquired.

"Hey Scott! I'm free in a few minutes. Where do you want

to meet? The Casino restaurant?" He asked.

" Yeah! That's cool. We'll have some coffee.

" I think I'm going to join you on that flight." Scott told him.

See you in a few. He hang up the phone.

Scott headed to the motel. When he arrived he took a seat in the restaurant. He must've waited 15 minutes before Allen arrive.

He walked into the entranceway and Scott stood up. Allen recognized him and walked over the table. The two of them shook hands and sat down.

"So what do you have for me"? Allen asked.

" Our suspect Mrs Franklin packed up and cut out with the doctor. I sat in your office and tracked him down. Their on a plane to Bermuda .

They left this morning they are ahead of you. I don't know what they're up to but we need to get there. What time is your flight."Scott asked.

"My flight leaves here at 4:30. I need to go pick a few bags at the house. I can meet you back at the airport."

Scott agreed. They had their coffee and left.They arrived in the terminal and parked the car. They went into the airport to the front desk.

They were informed that the flight was canceled due to the coronavirus. More than half the flights going out of the country were canceled. They were confused as to what to do. They left the airport and went back to the station. The two of them walked into the Chiefs office. He was told what happened.

The Chief was disappointed that they couldn't get out. The only thing they can do is call the Royal Bermuda Regiment. Alert them of what's going on. The Department could investigate the facts. It was the Chief's recommendation .

They did exactly what the Chief had requested. The British Command were very receptive. They took down all the pertinent information including the address to the building.

The officer that was handling it was Martinez. He told Allen that he would be back in touch with him. The investigation would be completed as requested. The conversation ended.

Officer Martinez did not move fast on the case. It took him three days before he had an investigator dispatched . Two Officers went out to the address. There were construction workers behind the house   They pulled up and exited the car. They walk to the back of the house and confronted the foreman.

"Sir! Martinez said loudly.

The gentleman turned around and looked at him. He spoke in French and asked Martinez. "What can I help you with?"

"What are you doing out here? I have to hold this project up."Martinez told him.

The foreman look confused and asked him." Why?"

"We believe there's a body buried underneath the soil here. We're going to tape off the area. You are ordered to stop working. You need to pack up and get off of the property.

Before you leave I want you to give my partner all the names and addresses of your workers including yourself. Don't leave without giving him that information." Martinez told him.

Martinez had called into the office. He asked them to send out contractors to dig up to unearth these bodies.

While they were waiting he taped off the area. There was no cement poured to form the foundation. It made it accessible to be dug out. They were still framing other parts to be cemented.

Martines was happy there was no concrete on top of the earth. He walked around and looked at the earth. It didn't appear to be unsettled or touched. It was quite level.

" I don't think there's anything is buried here. He called the other officer over. What do you think? Does it look like this has been tampered with?" He asked.

It don't look that way to me. It hasn't been played with in about two or three weeks. That would be my guess! You can see the foot prints from the workers and the topsoil. If it was played with it would be soft on top. He told Martinez.

A new group of construction workers had just arrived. There were seven of them that pulled up in an old truck. They walked into the yard and confronted Martinez.

"What do we need to do?"
The foreman asked?

"I want you to take the backhoe and dig up the dirt between the forms. We believe there's a body buried underneath the earth. They were going to pour cement and seal it underneath.

The contractors fired up the backhoe and pulled it towards the forms. The operator carefully dug into the earth. He dug deep in the soil and hit clay. He dug 6 feet and still nothing.

Martinez told him to stop. He walked back to the operator. He told the driver to fill the hole. There's nothing buried here."

(Act X).   Martinez and his partner return back to the station. He sat down at his desk and called Allen . He told him the news what transpired. He described how it dug down 6 feet between the forms and found nothing.

 Allen was just startled . He couldn't figure out how there was nothing there. He put his hand over the phone and told

Scott. Scott looked at him very confused .

"Good job Martinez. At least we know the band isn't there. I can't figure out what happened to it. Did you get the names of the addresses of the construction workers?" He asked Martinez.

I have all the information and the workers. I will fax them over to you. They concluded the conversation and hung up the phone.

Allen turned and looked at Scott. What the hell is going on here? Where we lied to? There were four people that's told the same story. What happened to the body? Allen questioned.

This is what I see Scott reply. I think the doctor and Hilda flew down there to warn those contractors. The contractors went to the house and unearthed the bodies. They relocated it somewhere.

We won't know until we find that doctor and his lady friend.

We need to call the airport and see if they have a flight back. When they do will meet them. They should have flights coming out of Bermuda to the states.

Scott began calling to check the ships. They have to come back here.

The British Government is asking all Americans to return to the homeland. I heard that on the way back from the airport on the radio.

"We have to find them. That's the bottom line". Allen replied. Scott told Allen.

 "There's no sense in me staying here any longer. There's nothing more we can do today. I'm going to go back to the motel. I will be here for a few more days.

 I'm going to put a stake out at the house. If he comes back I will nab them. If they don't come back in a couple days we're screwed.

The case will go cold. But at least we have the others charged. I know will get a conviction."

"We'll definitely get a conviction. I would say this

investigation looks stopped for now. That's my thought." Allen said.

Scott was about to leave the office when the phone rating. Allen pick up the phone and he answered. It was Martines.

"Allen I have some news for you." He said.

"What is that Martinez?" Allen responded.

"Two Officers went and talk to the neighbors across the street. This morning the contractors unearthed something from that yard. The neighbors witnessed them take out whatever was.

It was put into the back of their truck. They were warned we were coming. They took that body and relocated it. This is my thought." Martinez told Allen.

"I think you're right. Two people involved in the investigation took a plane to Bermuda today. We don't know where they're at. We're going to start looking for them. I'm going to give you some information on them.

Put in APB out. Maybe you could pick them up. I'll fax that information with mug shots to you. Get back to me if you hear anything. Allen said goodbye and hung up the phone.

The investigation went on for months. They were never located. Scott went back to Tennessee and Allen was assigned to another case.

To be continued.
"Call The Thrill Killers"

Don't miss out on these great manuscripts.

"Call The Thrill Killers"
 ISBN:9798638452278

Order It Today!
Amazon. Com.
Call direct! 1-888-280-4331

Murder in Franklin County
Murder in Clark County
The Case Of Lily Garland
The Floating Cemetery
Men For Justice
Call The Thrill Killers